three towels (We PAN ACROSS t ... one moth-eaten blanket. But su ... given the weight of her collection. Twelve-foot shelves lined the main room. She owned a lot of books but the shelves held objects. Idols. Instruments. Tools. (QUICK FLASH to: penis gourd) Fossils. Photographs. Coast Salish baskets. Familiar cans in unreadable scripts. I got used to sleeping underneath her spear. [INT. APARTMENT – NIGHT] (ARCHIVIST and ANTHROPOLOGIST on mattress; no bed frame) It was that distinctive mix of colours and textures. (STOCK SHOT: Afghani rug featuring tanks and camels) Anthropologists' homes are predictably eclectic. Petite museums. But this isn't the evidence that matters. [INT. POLICE DEPARTMENT INTERVIEW ROOM – DAY] They're writers. Occasionally the prose is a bit dispassionate – try stripping all the affect out of the scene of a genocide. INVESTIGATOR: How long did this arrangement continue? (Places arrangement in quotation marks with fingers) (Chuckles) ARCHIVIST: For over a decade. I'd drive to New York the day before her departure. (QUICK FLASH to: Taconic Parkway) We'd spend the night together. [INT. APARTMENT – DAWN] Then, she'd just leave. Sometimes for a month – once for nearly a year. Not many share her expertise or (INSERT: ANTHROPOLOGIST shackled on dirt floor of holding cell) tolerance for prolonged periods of discomfort. At some point there'd be a call or email.

(DISSOLVE to: computer) (We PAN ACROSS archivist's inbox and scroll down screen) I used to leave before she arrived, but once was still there in my pyjamas. We never talked about it. After that, I always waited. She never said a word. Just dropped her bags and headed for the shower. I'd cook (FLASH to: Thai in cardboard) or order in. Wait. She was completely withholding for the first four or five hours, but this didn't stop her from asking questions. She'd ask about my latest acquisition. Whose papers. What restrictions. What gossip. She'd ask about other things too. Had they raised the price of a MetroCard? Had her building been bombed for roaches lately? She was pragmatic despite the ill-equipped kitchen and lack of linens. [INT. POLICE DEPARTMENT INTERVIEW ROOM – DAY] INVESTIGATOR: Did she ever talk about her work? ARCHIVIST: Usually it would take at least a bottle of wine and a few shots of scotch. That's when I'd ask her to start reading. It was a bit ritualistic. Of course, she respected rituals. [EXT. RWANDAN VILLAGE – DAY] She'd travelled around the world immersing herself in passages. (CLOSE ON: funeral cloth tied around the anthropologist's wrists and neck) That much was obligatory. Why she could do this work. Why people fell in love with her too. But she was quite a rough-looking woman. Smelled of the business. I got to know this over the course of our relationship. It was never exclusive. We didn't talk about who else she fucked, how she defined – I was just a subletter. A body conducting a series of turbulent departures and arrivals. (QUICK FLASH to: ANTHROPOLOGIST throwing glass against wall) It was mutually convenient for reasons I won't go into here. But after the scotch, she'd go to her bag and retrieve a notebook. Moleskin. Spiral bound. Sketch pad. They were always different. Oddly, she preferred grids to lines. SMASH TO END OF TEASER, ROLL TITLE CREDITS

Fieldnotes
a forensic

Kate Eichhorn

BookThug | Toronto | MMX

Cover image: *Liquid City* (detail) 2006, by Simonetta Moro. Phototransfer, oil and encaustic on paper mounted on canvas; tape on wall, 50 canvases 11"x14" each, dimension variable. Private collection, Italy. Used with permission.

The production of this book was made possible through the generous assistance of The Canada Council for The Arts and The Ontario Arts Council.

Canada Council for the Arts   Conseil des Arts du Canada   ONTARIO ARTS COUNCIL   CONSEIL DES ARTS DE L'ONTARIO

LIBRARY AND ARCHIVES CANADA CATALOGUING IN PUBLICATION

Eichhorn, Kate
        Fieldnotes, a forensic / Kate Eichhorn.

Poems.

ISBN 978-1-897388-66-2

        I. Title.

PS8609.I28F53 2010   C811'.6   C2010-905580-2

Could it be that with disembodiment, presence expands? Language is like that too.

– Michael Taussig

SCENE I.

[Int. Apartment - Night] (We PAN ACROSS card-indexes, a travel diary, anthropological notes, maps, diagrams and photographic negatives)

One perfect autumn day I attended 11 funerals
people lined the street awaiting loved ones with open graves
I stood behind a middle-aged man

"If you cared, you wouldn't carry a thin blade
between villages," a pseudonymic photograph of my dead
who touched me on the shoulder

wished I could give him 1000 marks
some answers

Most people spilled with foreignness
this weekly harvest of respects provided closure

"How'd he die?" I looked at my clipboard
answered, "There were landmines
in the nature of these injuries"

I craft these freshly dug statements

to investigate our consumption of fear

repatriate the impossibility of war

I drove from village to village with my ethnic-cleansing methodology
an onlooker tells me in a language I do not speak
"You do not see because you have units of analysis
such as states"

The purpose of this text was dutifully transcribed
with incomprehensible force
taken by the reader dilettante day-tripping
in another body's funeral

For those who had given us permission
obligation boiled to write
for the exhumed

but decomposition has never been
a picturesque rural village under thunder

This is a bodily observation
the most radical of all ideas

not far from where we were indiscriminate in a sunlit clearing
the world unfolds

always inscribed on my knowledge-producing warfare
an obligation to other bodies

personification into units behind artillery
result of perfect planning

Ethnographic frailties or the failing of fieldnotes. Trying ruminations troubling my informants: (some) other ill-powerful society. I felt a responsibility to revise "my village" and to "get it right." Best draw unveiling their secrets. Conflicted piecing of voices. Contexts. Aristocratic clans. The women "animals" admitted to quotation marks. ~~Academic mentors stress objectivity~~ Authoritarian regimes control our ~~patronizing indulgence~~ barbarian ignorance. The indignant, domineering, wryly amused recording of data. The voice here is clearly that – a form of implicit public shamanism. Being experimental with form, analysis, perspective or interpretation of Society X was discouraged. Society X accepted there was a style of presentation within which I had to work. Their daily lives a few days of vivid research. I would not impose my impressionist desires on Society X's clear and hard material culture. Society X would not expect me to render them beautiful after a mudslide or bout of tribal warfare. But few initiates eat flesh or maintain control. Decidedly aberrant, carefully worded and often embarrassing understandings (secular insights) reveal secrets – mental illness, spirit loss. This study was meant to be haunted by effaced cosmologies. Threads warping already-speaking local crowds. But life utterly sacred and freezing seeks her own canopy epistles. Naturally, also the exegesis of miracles. Return to meaning. My public outbursts damage this quickly-hustled fieldworker telling of village ~~life~~ death and her authority. Each text calling for communal possession.

ANTHROPOLOGIST: (Whispering) This really happened. Once, smelling like dust up in rib cages. Months of bodies. Some laid out on cafeteria trays. (QUICK FLASH to: armband made of human hair and mystical clarinet consisting of a small feathered gourd) It was strange. They were that tiny. Then the slip. It's calming to use epithets on occasion, but this time I wept, diminishing in the arms of an intern.

11:00 pm, trawling surfaces
aerial catch in a cove

     skin slippage
     gloving
     remains in a holding pattern

10:45 am, 15,000 pieces
 sold-out freezer bags

 volunteers praised
  the revival in canning

Cross-legged scribbling clusters of sea oats. The cusp between jumbled and gasping. Nothing substantiated. Ascertained. Deprivation experiments started this. I pictured cross-border treks and their symptoms. Excavating. Fame. Wearing opaque goggles. Anxiety. Some depression. Hallucinating forward, the interminable diversions. It's a specialized world – mutilated, inwardly groaning. For me, the attraction was its dismembered branches.

ANTHROPOLOGIST: (Eating with fingers) I don't know why this was rejected by Communications? (QUICK FLASH to: dark and airless cubicles suited neither for rest, leisure nor love) I was asked to give a testimony for the university website. Tell us, in your own words, why you pursued this career. So I gave them the cusp between jumbled and gasping. Nothing substantiated. Ascertained. Deprivation experiments. Depression. Dismembered branches. They wanted something to SELL my program. I THOUGHT this summed it up – the exotic locations, smell of decay, primacy of writing alongside the presence of specimens, the impact on your social life (We PAN ACROSS the filth, chaos, congestion; ruins, huts, mud, dirt, dung, urine, pus, humours, secretions, running sores) and the interdisciplinary nature of the field. What's-her-name sent an email saying it was a bit too poetic and negative for the website. Asked me to write something more scientific and upbeat. (Greasy hand seizes glass) I refused. Told her it was taken straight from my notebooks infused with all the affects of the field. (FLASH to: ANTHROPOLOGIST dazed, debilitated, playing with the dead, dancing) She rewrote it on my behalf: "Imagine yourself lying on the beach at the end of a hard day's work. Sun beating down, you record your observations. Part scientist, part Gandhi and part Kathy Reichs, (QUICK FLASH to: painted old hag laden with pendants) the forensic anthropologist is highly objective, compassionate and creative, and in a world teeming with natural and human tragedy, always in demand." They published that over a full-page sepia-toned photograph of me crawling into a cave – all ass, no head! [INT. DEAN'S OFFICE – DAY] INSERT: VISUALIZATION (ANTHROPOLOGIST crushing the occupant under an indifferent mass of stones)

SCENE II.

[Int. Apartment–Night]   (We PAN
ACROSS the ANTHROPOLOGIST
and ARCHIVIST watching each
other and trying to avoid possible
social blunders)

"Methodological competence" assumes you see "it." A would-be sorcerer's mind resisting spirits moved from cultural means to cool down. There's some dirt on my observations but no difference. Met a touched-the-ground guide. Precarious still played an important part structuring borders breached, but crossing with an affable conversationalist, people soon become convivial. It's always a transgression of sorts (I'll be able to say this more easily leaving) to work on the confines of unsavory outright conflict. Repulsive, yes, but rather here than a factory. That's one explanation. Still, it's a series of tiny, repetitive, much-like-living gestures.

ANTHROPOLOGIST: (Intoxicated) I'm not making pro-
clamations, but I am developing a slim theory of people.
The story of the hospital in the hands of the army. The
story of one bullet executing two cities. The story of ghost
towns. The stress of evil surrounding the refuge. (With
a vegetable regularity by which Baudelaire would have
been pleasantly surprised) The story of beautiful danger.
Following the harshness and attacks, record my thoughts.
Shoving one another is a chance for life. An asymmetrical
quench.

9:40 am, Said she'd take a toothbrush over a comb
some brought razors or eclectic biological relics

> 3 Tupperwares of nail clippings
> 47 stained butts
> a snorkel

Not much to say about Ziplocing traces of an empire's ablutions

*

10:15 am, Feelings enhance the chaos of this variable-rich
investigation

12:45 pm, Never rush a monk skinning corpses on a precipice

Recalling the vulture's patience scan for signs of yak butter
barley

Dwarfed by height a street may appear uninhabitable

Replace vultures with carp, release the bone shards riverside
birds think they're just eating, so do fish

Sipping tea from a frontal bone?   doubted

You can tread softly on a corpse with one foot coverage
no such precaution in a soiless field

Had I imagined hoisting cherished remains into the crown
canopy?

There was no trace of *tsampa*

5:15 pm, Descended and marvelled, nothing more enviable
than the dermestidae's fine finishing work

Never dreamt this elevator trip to the field

Burnt-out retina realizing I'd never seen tissue in the field
(narrowly missed a mummified infant
helping DMORT rescue a graveyard)

Stress is key to form: two decades on three continents helped
separate plastic forks from notched fragments

Still prefer it prone, straddling a single, fragile companion, arms
barely reaching the lumbar

3:40 am, A minor figure in an exorbitant expenditure
recording every angle but "minor figure" knows
a thing or two about shamanism and a scrotum or toe

Scarcity of white skin on the table masked the tone
demanding scraps in reception

Takes a machine to translate cartilage to barcode

Writing in the face of that data made me vulnerable. Cursed my uterus. Troubled, I became a client to a healer. A practitioner of sorts. We had varied and tentative identifications based on our shared status. (Perhaps I should leave it there? I'm departing the realm of rational conduct). There were insights, findings, magic, even specimens. Sorcery was used to label some of the photographs. The text we anticipated was entirely accurate. He already knew because presence is grounded on the fate of a tableau. On the contrary, I only contributed memories, interruptions, negative affects.

ANTHROPOLOGIST: They air-dropped a digital micro-scope and medicine. I learned how to clean the equipment with a tooth brush. (DISSOLVE to: ANTHROPOLOGIST lying in a corner of her hut with a very high temperature) Hostile and alien, the lump was palpable. Mysteriously, soon evacuated.

Irony's edge blunted in the choking stench, violence stalks
victims, even at the morgue

Morbid interchange for unidentified remains
dredged from fetid swales

Flesh swells in a back alley pooling with mysterious septic
substances

Army's surplus: most primitive form of accumulation

White suits zip bloodied, disfigured bodies into black bags
chorus line for –

With refrigerator capacity for 100, morgue's 1-month guarantee
indefinitely on hold

How can blackened skeletons live with this shrapnel
splattered on walls?

The blast's nationalities were sheared off leaving a charred claim

"You can't be a wall of fear policing outposts across worry"

Occasionally a person is sufficiently close
completely disintegrated

From the moment meeting the biblical landscape, don't rule out
shock
                    lethal reflexes

Decapitated component in sandals clutching a transparent
folder   returns to scene

Excerpt from *Corpse Trading Places**

The body was taken and the stricken wife stated
"Police delivered it to another party?"

It's not difficult to exchange individuals or wares
since monopolizing public streets and a huge refrigerator

They followed a stream of blood to bury these bodies
on the 17th day of Ramadan leaving a dark red line
from La Belle Province to the outskirts of Baghdad

When the phone rang, he politely told the wife
"My friend stores bodies to fulfill his Shari'ah duty
respectful of the month, don't judge his profession low
there's 650,000 and counting, we're open to offers"

The husband raised a critical question: US 10,000
for families of victims because they're merciful

* Forthcoming novel by Charity Stahl.

ARCHIVIST: So you know Stahl? ANTHROPOLOGIST: (With strange inflection) I know she was raised by bank robbers. After their arrest, she endured a cycle of foster homes. She was socially awkward and emotionally distant but determined. By 31, she was already a successful forensic anthropologist. Spends her vacations volunteering in war zones and working on her bestselling series of (INSERT: cannibalism and necrophagy) crime novels. I've always found her irritating to work with (DISSOLVE to: ANTHROPOLOGIST descending into the bowels of the earth) when she bothers to show up at all. It's usually a cheap publicity stunt and deeply distracting to have her there with a Time Magazine photographer peering into the pit. Quite frankly, it's downright insulting to the family of victims who have no idea who she is but think writing thrillers about their dead is a huge taboo. (QUICK FLASH to: STAHL writing bestsellers and lecturing to packed halls) She hasn't kept up with developments in the field, but it's the writing I take offense to. I tried reading one of her fucking novels on a 22-hour flight. Even trapped in a metal tube, I couldn't bear to the structure of her sentences INSERT: VISUALIZATION (STAHL immersed for a long period in icy water) (Lying on the bare ground)

(Swarming with maggots) END: VISUALIZATION and don't get me started about her stilted dialogue. Then, once, I got drunk after a hellish day in the field (FLASH to: corpse in grave covered with branches) and she was there. I lost it. Two years later showed up in her next novel. Name changed, but it was obviously me as a crazed loner chasing mass graves. (We PAN ACROSS a web of temptations, provocations, enticements and reprisals) I could have sued. Read it yourself – Grave Encounter. Stupid title for a book about duelling forensic anthropologists.

SCENE III

[Int. Apartment - Dusk] (STOCK
SHOT: clothing and blankets)

ANTHROPLOGIST: Not yet. (INSERT: big cock) Archivist: Fine. It's not like I've been waiting for (STOCK SHOT: the most favourable spot) three months. ANTHROPOLOGIST (Explained by means of gestures): So you fuck other women in my bed when I'm gone? ARCHIVIST: There was a fledgling attorney (We PAN ACROSS joints smaller than generally the case) so if you want to formalize this arrangement, I'll ask her to stipulate the terms before your next appointment with death. ANTHROPOLOGIST: Cunt! (QUICK FLASH to: objects – a stick, a pestle) That's how you see it? ARCHIVIST: Yes. (FLASH to: beaten white bark passed between the thighs) ANTHROPOLOGIST: Fuck you! ... uh, a bit lower, no ... shit, you're out of practice! ARCHIVIST (Harnessed and loaded): Everyone has their preference, and yes, it's bad form to transpose (FLASH to: toy) them across lovers. ANTHROPOLOGIST: You're not the only one who plays the field. There was a cute local this time but too young and (STOCK SHOT: overheated ship, a mixture of sea smells, whiffs) too butch. ARCHIVIST: Since when have you been so fucking ethical? As if! What about the girl you – ANTHROPOLOGIST (Beginning to glow): There ... no, yes – there ... and yes, I am so fucking ethical – fuck yes! ARCHIVIST (gazing): Ethics is all about (QUICK FLASH to:

upper arms or ankles) the other. Shit, you haven't been fucked in over three months, have you? It's (CLOSE ON: no more than a straw tassel hanging from a belt above the sexual organs) obvious. ANTHROPOLOGIST: Shut the fuck up! ARCHIVIST: Am I disturbing your little too young, too butch local (INSERT: drunk with secretions) fantasy, my dear? ANTHROPOLOGIST: If you must know (We PAN ACROSS an enclosure reminiscent of some Normandy stud farm) fuck yes!

SCENE IV.

[Int. Apartment – Dawn] (We PAN
ACROSS hollow, feeble shadows like
the flat of some stage set)

6:45 am, Awake since 4
nestled in soil and undergrowth
all this taken in stride as stable personalities work the pit
another day of eyelashes
liquefying colour of cloth slings
maggots

This is the power of hair adhering in chunks
to skulls

7:20 am, Still no breakfast, game face for the job
indifferent feelings

I look three hundred years old
mindset allows me to approach this scene
much like short-grass cattle country
where I grew up

emotional chain of custody
breaking down only in the shadow
of rain

3:27 pm, Reality of the last hours
4 interviews of the dead with children
enigmatic thick testimonies
(rubbed underarm deodorant on my face mask)
slumpage of the visible

*

7 pm, The irretrievable finality of leaving behind my shovels
(as if they also saw the destruction I'm now accepting)

After a full day I go back to my room. Reflect upon wet tarmac and glistening cassava. Every peak. Core reason I decided to cram into that bus. Disembarked to ~~discover~~ breathe in this mood – anticipation carpets short gasps. Tattered tarpaulins over some of the windows gave the impression of stalled work. After a full day of rain, something ominous – the sun broke through foreboding. I reflected off to the side of the wet tarmac under the drooping plantain leaves. This was the core reason I decided to go along the road. The mood was reflexive. Upbeat with a tinge of anticipation. Crammed into a single bus, a propaganda machine populated by authorities, one-dimensional misery. They unlatched my discipline certain my presence was anchored in a type of fetishization or reconstruction of the exotic. The warm gust of backwardness. Against the wall, don't get me wrong, I hovered over their little "bloodlust" and "book learning" comment. Rich and varied created this chain of events from wall to community. Wall to wall. Doves flapped around pure and abstract eliciting expressionism. The "caretakers" of the visiting anthropologists delivered 100 questions. The record *shouldn't* be academic theory. It's important to recognize the inner workings of the group. Your colonial tinge. To integrate the unique understandings of the military. The way *we* view ecological knowledge and practice. Applied work without theorizing. Anthropologists' public way of glossing over-simplified pseudo-scientific data.

ANTHROPOLOGIST: (Overexcited) It was the early 1990s (QUICK FLASH to: ANTHROPOLOGIST with pierced nasal septum) and we were thick in the midst of the appropriation debates. I'll never forget the weekly hell of "Women, Power and Imperialism." I was already well versed in the ascent from structuralist imperatives to colonial impositions (INSERT: "going native") but this wasn't an anthropology class. It was something interdisciplinary and full of women (STOCK SHOT: women dressed as men simulating processions of warriors) one absolutely stunning and hell-bent on attacking me (SUPER: shop-girl metaphysics) weekly. She was writing a thesis derivative of Trinh T. Minh-ha's fashionable assault on the profession, and I was her "White Cancer." (FLASH to: Rousseau thinking the 'contract'.) Demanded account for centuries of violence before I'd even entered the field, but she was brilliant. [INT. CONJUGAL ABODE – NIGHT] (We PAN ACROSS the ANTHROPOLOGIST – wrists, arms, calves, and ankles bound) Now she chairs a Philosophy program at an elite four-year college. Occasionally complains about the lack of diversity but loves the prestige and benefits package. I thought about her crammed into that single bus (MONTAGE: PHILOSOPHER and ANTHROPOLOGIST in the

Colorado Rockies, suburbs of Rio and streets of New York)
certain my presence was anchored in a type of fetishization
or reconstruction of the exotic and deeply grateful she'd
given me all the right answers.

Trance states, disruptions, distally traumatic "twilight zones" – *emic* explanations, i.e., cultural ancestors, traditional devils, outsiders and miscellaneous spirits, cross my "naturalistic" diagnostic categories. These syndromes are all schemes developed to easily capture a catharsis or "time-out" from a stressful situation. Sudden death. Catastrophe. Prolonged puzzlement. We've all been "crazy" from *that* point of view. Reported a loss of fine-turning. Unravelling dynamics. Preponderance. The interplay between personality functions. I've suffered from sleep disturbances. Prodromal brooding. "Normal" depression. Withdrawal. Anxiety. Depersonalization. Delusions. Thought amnesia. Thanatomania. Mutism. Empowering force syndrome. Echopraxia (taboo and normal). Echolalia. Glossolalia. Paroxysm. Other malignant verbal developments. A tour of the world expressed in symptoms. Syndromes. Explanations for unimaginable events. Therapy can include drink. Complete isolation. Knotted strings around necks. Blood boiled for steam. Childbirth. Thrashing. Counteragents. Coins. The meat of certain animals. Rich tobacco smoke. Muttering. Charms. Purging. Dramatizations. A calabash of water or convulsed tongue of a healer. Complete loss of control over Western nosology.

10:45 am, A sort of fool's errand in an abattoir
we found burnt bone, keys and a watch strap

*

4:15 pm, Silently carry buckets of the mine-removal specialist
families watch

Someone tells blackened soil how they died
(me?)

Opening shallow lines, beach-toy-size shovel out the hills
to bury them

Mentions in public discourse were peripheral ellipses. There was a refusal to contribute. To celebrate their lives. Eulogize the unacknowledged. Their deaths. Attending to these losses, survivors felt the pressure of biographical details. A memorial path of imperatives. The need to articulate intimate, lain-open reasons for the "missing." Theories of why they'd been ignored. Template eulogist language typically excludes bodies. Experiences of criminality. The commonplace gestures of death. I know this genre and its conventions – we're-all-close-normalcy and the domesticity of daughters (no broken homes, notoriety or victims-of-a-serial-killer). Euphemisms help conform to these generic expectations. Render loads of how-it-should-be families celebrating life in death. This sort of text blends together the remembered. Junkies, hookers and homeless-with-a-heart-of-gold victims are left significantly empty. Abstract. A few even exemplary. Obliquely encircled by blank ideas, after large-scale tragedies the dead as poster people do something to ensure never again. It's equal to posthumous stamping.

11:30 pm, 10,000 litres of raw sewage in buckets ignited waves
of fury
around the septic tank sieved
for the solid matter
of sisters

I have fantasies of the trench end
dunking you in

ANTHROPLOGIST: That's really what moves people. Matters of status. I walk straight into a village missing half its mothers and everyone's mourning the blue-balled. (FLASH to: the fertility of gardens and women) A bit crass to say, but priorities in a tragedy aren't always about what lies beneath the shrouds. Women deal. (INSERT: a certain structural pattern) Lack of lack's another story.

SCENE V.

[Int. Apartment – Night]
(We PAN ACROSS the claustro-
phobic, Turkish-bath atmosphere
imprisoned by the practice of
philosophical reflection)

Label	Standpoint		

Label	**Standpoint**	
(A) Specimens ⟶	~~Anthropologist~~	Spy
(B) Bones ⟶	~~Fieldworker~~	Traitor
(C) Dogs ⟶	~~Scoundrel~~	Leader
(D) Heritage ⟶	~~Historian~~	Liar
(E) Tibia ⟶	~~Pathologist~~	Collaborator
(F) Lovers ⟶	~~Victim~~	Shit
(G) Evidence ⟶	~~Investigator~~ ~~Poet~~	Do-gooder
(H) Children ⟶	~~Parent~~	Dirt
(I) Artifacts ⟶	~~Curator~~	Thief

Preoccupation with the sanctity of borders is loosely termed a "mass casualty." A symptom of practices. We were swimming transients who scarcely spoke in these "ways." Sought tutelage in a multiplicity of screen and print coverage fiercely competing over incidents. The unquestioned reliance on points of the body. Littered and overturned boxes of fruit. Splattered vegetables. The three-phase process of loss, chaos and regathering usually in a calm tone with vivid description. A story titled "Marketplace blends a daughter's body with gun powder, spices and pickles." Ripped of bodily idioms of loss and disorder, hundreds of volunteers swarm wrapped in shrouds. Ritual of entering another tragic "mass disaster." This didn't alter the fact that we were there. Leaping into bathtubs. Frequently into – the researcher will always be entering. Like this? To spot. Transcribe. Impeccably covered. Seamless. Totally integrated. A whole diminishing process. Just-like-anyone, the fieldworker melts into obligations manifested in hardships. Endured rapport. The same concrete manifestations and autobiographical details.

Spectral analysis and faith led me to your checkpoint

legibility of a fractal signature or soccer field
could be our battleground

more than pens slip where bucket loaders gouge the hillside

no erasing signatures visible at 10,000 feet

Those natal boys were a metaphor the village provided me, insisting they *were* the victims. I accepted this but worried about the essentials of patriotic martyrdom. It's never neutral (decapitation). It always remains a display of heads. Writing of any kind is a complex ~~matter~~ encounter. Children screaming strategic choices while men scramble active constructions. What to omit? Whose voices? What metaphors raised by grief? How much recall returned with an insider's passionate bereavement? These are the exotic, tricky and prominent features of eavesdropping.

3 soldiers bore arms on crutches
2 navigated the field with canes
1 brought a toy gun to battle

they chose a soccer field as their battleground
why combat boots not cleats?

Some come forth from sacrament to puzzlement. Prior to dramatic arguments and killing, neighbours embraced. Looked ethical. An "I-you" could bridge a conversation. The abyss between. But there was a compelling disparity. "He or she is *not* military." The faceless man labelled "terrorism" is? Discourses couched in many ways. Political-cum-religious persons orchestrated strategies. Constructions of violence. Containment. Looking into dragons (I-antagonisms), humanity was plagued by the generated perplexity of its actors. Order by means of competition is fierce, but there's a utopian element in genocide. The routine nature of having no face. That's perplexing. Bonding all of us, a desire to narrative-capture the very essence of a good burlesque satire or ethnography. Whether it searches for redemption or catastrophe, there are definitional problems. Style *pre*figures factual information. I felt impotent to stop this. In words, "lightly equipped." Grew deeply distressed. Unanswerable. Glorified. Dehumanized. It was impossible to know ourselves and to carry on.

Signature	Sign
Sneakers	Identification mark
Tire tracks	Identification mark
Weaponry	Violence
Cartridge	Violence
Odour	Body
Empty wallet	Identification mark
Foreign soil	Relocation
Missing hair	DNA
Fingernails	DNA
Ramping	Mass grave
Teeth marks	Mass grave
Disarticulation	Disturbance

ANTHROPOLOGIST: Mostly, I don't write about things witnessed. (INSERT: the usual ideological weapon used by oligarchies to combat personal power) It's true. No data. No identification marks. Nothing but that gasp or lurch coming into an encounter. Not (INSERT: gigantic strides without the help of writing) much. Not really.

Spent the night launched against the landscape documenting the distance. Came down when a voice shouted over the projectiles. Baked bread filled a narrow alley. An old man transformed lay strewn on the ground. I became air. Went inside. Breathable told two arbitrary figures about the expulsion and need to hide. They told me to speak louder. Be careful. We buzz like sound too exposed, but I knew how to take notes with *total* indifference. Shot their nearly imperceptible steps at close range. Physical prowess. Stomachs. Sobs. Ripped wounds in their brutal narrow hallways. There was no wall there. No protest. Single file entering ties arrived. I heard the voice of bodies on top of moans. Cells took the weight. Sound spreading across the floor. The torture of ears. That we move is nothing small. Chests. Backs. My head in a pool of black boots. Hand signals and signs. Dispassionately, shoulders and thighs. My eyes. Teeth. Chin tilting. This unaffected grasp. You never really know your arms. Being held is a looseness. A sinking into. I expected her to leave abruptly. To kick. My body separated. Hands begged for form. Compassion's gesture opening moments between a gaze. I fell into a small room where women were evident. Asleep. Slow. Deformed. To list a few uncovered faces. Again to separate. Put my jacket back over my head. Bruises on my chest as declarations. Voices shouting. The typewriter out front was calling my name. I went to document what happened. Every moment. Every alias. Every face. The atmosphere. This clenched cigarette. A stiffness and resistance. Entwined with the *Apocalypse Now* theatre there's a Wordsworthian narrative that will unwind over the empty territories. Make it pertinent. We were fingerprinted to record our statements.

SCENE VI.

[Int: Apartment – Night] (CLOSE ON the ANTHROPOLOGIST heavy with patience, serenity and mutual forgiveness that, through some involuntary understanding, one can sometimes exchange with a cat)

Walking straightforward with buoyancy my legs didn't tire coming here, but my hands hurt quickly. What breaks out of the cuff area, shoulders, thumbs. Hyperextending postures. It's this deskwork. Stretching case by case the flexion of notes. This index flipping the memory into different lived moments (the giving up, resentment, checkpoints where I grasped myself again). Fieldwork necessarily includes failures in reconstruction. Also excessive pleasures. Confusion. Today it was the expression of an absent field. The women gave me means (not memories or dates). Lower bodies vis-à-vis shoulders. Memories vis-à-vis hips. A network of palms. The inner surfaces of fingers. Viscerally stepping beyond the sway of order, proprioceptive more than visual, I felt the weight of reading these patterns. Monitoring forearms down routes. Distal ends leading toward paths. The gravity of conduct. Contact. A smile or gaze intricately twisted out from an upper torso. Ephemeral cairns. Unreadable. Still in motion I stretch to graph these principles. The density of this telling of subjects, objects, selves etc. "Eyes looking" (a learnable imitative act), objectivity buckles in the face of fallible multivocal absences. Today I couldn't even monitor my own blinking. Loosely described, every step felt the length of this entry. A coil of conditions for winding in many dimensions. Durations. A single and absorbing story made it possible to confront the bus terminal. Tea house half a mile away. The real issue was the emptiness. Her painful legs refused to emerge. It was a question of a particular movement. A passage from analyses to terrifying hallucination. The pressure oozing out of her. Still nursing, she held up the head. Her own singular sensation of pain. Ferociously archival proof of an event that left no other material. No dancing devils or spiteful stains. Crazed figures with bracelets, rings or intricate feather work. Acquiescence hides the rest. Combing documents, oral myths, Polaroids, dirt, toys, various circuits of memory between warm beer and food, she transmitted her separation in a large plastic bag. A tooth relic. Broken tip. The body was no longer rememberable. What it had been "before" under the influence and over the obstructions. Decisive unconscious complicities that mark the best of bodies. I came in time to surmount this. A compass of pale lines concluding cases I knew she was not herself on the dance floor. One can be everything there. Glimpse a body capable of escaping years. She came with a name attached re-enacting the paralysis of these events. A private theatre of impressions. The end of space. How small the choreographed repetition of symptoms. Periodic blindness. Catharsis. Again, the act of finding ourselves in a passage. A memoir. Narrating led me to heads located at the edge of interpretation. Fingernails cut with traumatic precision. Errors. Paretic emptiness. The intangible centre of identity breathes itself into my hands. Face alight I register her performance. The real occasion of hard-edged anguish. I did not steal anyone's details. Reputation. Attributes. These last three days spent the night in an interior garden. Identical notebooks with maps of the site. "Literary turn" on my mind, I looked down on all this from a single knoll. The white domed shrines. Crenulated walls. Abstract geometries. Caravanserais baths. The sensation of distinct vocabularies. One would think that to end should be easy. You just stop. How inconceivable body of the town tumbling across these incised lines.

ACKNOWLEDGEMENTS

This book was made possible with support from the Ontario Arts Council, Canada Council for the Arts and Lower Manhattan Cultural Council. I also wish to acknowledge *Filling Station, Matrix, PRECIPICe, Sugar Mule, EOAGH* and *Cultural Studies <=> Critical Methodologies* for publishing work in progress. For turning my manuscript into a book, I thank Jay MillAr and Jenny Sampirisi at BookThug, and for adding their own words and works, Simonetta Moro and Laura Mullen. Books can be surprisingly long in the making – I owe much to Celia Haig-Brown who first introduced me to the possibilities, limitations and poetics of ethnographic writing. Claude Lévi-Strauss owes special mention – his *Tristes Tropiques* was a source (STOCK SHOT: astonishing gallery) of directions throughout. Finally, this book was informed by ongoing dialogues with friends and colleagues. For insights, editorial feedback and other interventions I am grateful to Elena Basile, Emily Beall, Angela Carr, Margaret Christakos, Heather Milne, Akilah Oliver, Drake Patton, Rebecca Rosenberg, Gail Scott, Cheryl Sourkes, Taunya Tremblay and Rachel Zolf.

COLOPHON

Manufactured in an edition of 500 copies in the fall of 2010.
Distributed in Canada by the Literary Press Group WWW.LPG.
CA. Distributed in the United States by Small Press Distribution
WWW.SPDBOOKS.ORG. Shop on line at WWW.BOOKTHUG.CA

BOOK
PRODUCTION
WAR ECONOMY
STANDARD

Type + Design by Jay MillAr
Edited for the press by Angela Carr

Illuminated missing persons scene

cut to your jacket and hold

caption reads

stained panties breaking

FADE TO END OF TEASER reporter

turns to ROLL TITLE

close up on crowd

gather your mouth as you just beyond try to

crime scene tape YOU: "... ah"

have difficulty pronouncing these media frenzy words

extending the corpus

push your way through the Latin

FADE make your measuring way toward the barn

distance from backhoe driver's body

quick nearby flash of outdoor party

lean down pick up walking

look like a laminated birth glob of mud

CUT from a sole of WHITE FLASH

talk to the crowd

pull Polaroids off dissipated bulletin board

floodlights and hand it to you

CUE sweet Jane through bus station suitcase in her body

second time lapse and she looks on

STRIP woman with billboard looming

FADE IN: STOCK crimped hair

You're traveling past the

VARIOUS CUTS to her body

more time passes pulling her OPENING

MISSING you off to paradise

CSI his kit, her hair

DOE, JANE you point and nod

DOE, JANE using a crowbar

DOE, JANE another coroner

DOE, JANE a set of bones

DOE, JANE the examining table

DOE, JANE forensics

label side of DOE, JANE

formalin-fixed DOE, JANE

no traces of Ecstasy DOE, JANE

chloral hydrate DOE, JANE

morphology DOE, JANE

toe tag on table dials skeletal remains

JANE DOE'S RECORDED VOICE

CUE SONG

The real issue was the emptiness. Her painful legs refused to emerge. It was a question of a particular movement. A passage from analyses to terrifying hallucination. The pressure oozing out of her. Still nursing, she held up the head. Her own singular sensation of pain. Ferociously archival proof of an event that left no other material...

Kate Eichhorn's writing is miraculous: she can suggest a novella in a paragraph and invoke a solid narrative (compelling the suspension of disbelief) while drawing our attention to the medium itself – often in the same sentence – so that reading becomes a kind of lucid dreaming in which the pleasure of mimesis is in equipoise with the pleasure of seeing how mimesis works or fails to work. In destabilizing the "Standpoint" and distrusting the "Template eulogist language [that] typically excludes bodies," *Fieldnotes* catalogues mourning as it enacts a search for more trustworthy strategies of approach to love and loss. Equal parts thriller and experimental poem, this inquiry into the tragic consequences of failures of communication and community is also a hot exploration of desire. As delicious as it is difficult, as rigorous as it is original, inventive and various, this is a truly marvelous book. – LAURA MULLEN

KATE EICHHORN is the author of *Fond*, a finalist for the Gerald Lampert Award, and co-editor of *Prismatic Publics: Innovative Canadian Women's Poetry and Poetics*. Her poetry, prose and criticism are part of a serial investigation of historiography, ethnography and poetics. She teaches writing and cultural theory at The New School University in New York City.

$18.00

ISBN 978 1 897388 66 2